Disney · PIXAR

TOY STORY 2

A Junior Novel by Leslie Goldman

Disney PRESS

New York

The text for this book is set in 12-point ITC Garamond.
Library of Congress Catalog Card Number: 98-88404
ISBN 0-7868-4302-0

For more Disney Press fun, visit www.DisneyBooks.com

Chapter One

Buzz Lightyear sped through the dark sky, his blinking space suit lights flashing. He zeroed in on his target—a huge red planet. As the clouds surrounding the planet drifted away, he soared through, landing smoothly on the rocky surface. He raised his wrist communicator to contact his headquarters. "Buzz Lightyear mission log: all signs point to this planet as the location of Zurg's fortress." Buzz glanced up and down the surface of the deserted planet. "But there seems to be no sign of intelligent life anywhere."

Just as he was starting to relax, Buzz spotted a group of red laser beams. Seconds later, he was surrounded by armed robot forces. He raised his laser gun toward a crystal formation nearby and fired. A huge explosion blew the robots away. But he hadn't destroyed the enemy completely. From the wall of the crater, a robotic camera moved swiftly toward Buzz. He took aim once more and fired.

He was able to destroy the camera, but then he felt something shifting under his feet. Before he could move, the ground gave way beneath him, and he fell into a long, dark, deep cavern. Buzz landed on the ground, and spotted a maze. There was no other way to go, so he entered.

A blinking orange dot was on his back, though. The evil Zurg was monitoring Buzz's every step. "Come to me, my prey," Zurg growled from his control room.

Buzz walked through a door, and it closed behind him. Suddenly, deadly spikes shot out of the door, and zoomed toward Buzz. He ran down the tunnel and jumped through another door without a millisecond to spare. The spikes banged against the closed door, piercing the exterior. Buzz was safe for now. He treaded over a thin, swinging rope bridge with stealth, only to come face-to-face with Zurg.

"Buzz Lightyear! Your defeat will be my greatest triumph!" yelled Zurg, as he took aim with his ion blaster.

"Not today, Zurg," bellowed Buzz. He raised his shield, deflecting Zurg's bullet. Then he hurled the shield at Zurg, hitting him directly in the face.

Momentarily stunning Zurg, Buzz leaped over him, and fired one shot. It careened to Zurg's left, narrowly missing its target.

Zurg recovered and took aim again, blasting Buzz and blowing his torso off. "Ahh-ha-ha!" laughed a triumphant Zurg.

GAME OVER flashed in red across the screen.

Chapter Two

Andy Davis was out of sight, so his toys were playing on their own. The real Buzz Lightyear and his friend and fellow toy Rex, a plastic dinosaur, jumped up to the screen.

"Ooooh, now that's gotta hurt," Buzz said in sympathy.

Rex stomped his feet. "No! I'm never gonna defeat Zurg! I give up," he shouted.

"Come on. Pull yourself together, Rex. Remember, a Space Ranger must turn and face his fears no matter how ugly it gets. You must not flinch!"

"Okay, one more round," Rex said, ready to give it another try. He turned back to the TV screen. "Ah!" yelled Rex. Woody's sudden reflection across the video screen scared him.

Ignoring Rex's whimpering, Woody looked down at his magic erase clipboard and spoke to Buzz. "Okay, here's a list of things to do while I'm gone. Batteries need to be changed. Toys in the bottom of the chest need to be rotated. And make sure everyone attends Mr. Spell's seminar on 'what to do if you or a part of you is swallowed.' Okay?"

Buzz shook his head. "Woody, you haven't found your hat yet, have you?"

"No," said Woody. "Andy's leaving for cowboy camp any minute now, and I can't find it anywhere!"

"Don't worry. In just a few hours you'll be sitting around a crackling campfire with Andy making delicious hot schmoes," said Buzz.

"They're called s'mores, Buzz."

"Right," nodded Buzz. "Has anyone found Woody's hat yet?" he called to the rest of the toys.

Green Army Men swarmed around the open toy box. Some rappelled down from the open lid into the box. "Hut. Hut. Hut . . ." they chanted.

The sergeant approached Buzz and saluted. "Negatory. Still searching."

Hamm, the piggy bank, sat on the windowsill, looking outside through Lenny, the toy binoculars.

"The lawn gnome next door says it's not in the yard, but he'll keep looking," Hamm reported back.

Bo Peep and the Troll Doll walked into the room. "It's not in Molly's room. We've looked everywhere," shrugged Bo Peep.

Mr. Potato Head peeked out from under the bed. "I found it," he shouted.

"You found my hat?" cheered Woody.

"Your hat? Nah. The Mrs. lost her earring again. Oh, my little sweet potato?" He held up a plastic ear with a dangling earring attached.

Mrs. Potato Head walked up with a huge grin painted on her face. "You found it! It's so good to have a big strong spud around the house!" She took the ear and plugged it back in to her ear socket.

Woody walked over to Andy's packed duffel bags and kicked one of them. "Great. That's just great! This'll be the first year I miss cowboy camp, all because of my stupid hat."

"Woody, look under your boot," said Bo.

"Bo, don't be silly. My hat's not under my boot."

"Just look," she said.

Woody sighed, and then raised his foot and

looked at it. "There, see? No hat. Just the word *Andy*."

"Uh-huh," said Bo, smiling. "And the boy who wrote that would take you to camp with or without your hat."

Woody stared at the signature and smiled. Bo was right. "I'm sorry, Bo. It's just that I've been looking forward to this all year. It's my one time with just me and Andy."

Bo grinned, and snared Woody with the crook of her stick. She pulled him toward her. "You're cute when you care."

"Everyone's looking," whispered a blushing Woody.

"Let 'em look," she said, and kissed him.

Someone turned on the TV. A chicken clucking blared from the set. It was a commercial. A large man dressed in a chicken suit was flapping his wings atop Al's Toy Barn.

"Hey, kids," he clucked. "This is Al, from Al's Toy Barn. And I'm sitting on some good deals here . . . Ow! Ah think I'm feelin' a deal hatchin' right now! Let's see what we got!" The man squinted and squirmed, and then stood up to reveal a giant egg. It cracked open and a giant dollar bill appeared on the screen. A bunch of toys floated across the screen. "We got boats for a buck, beanies for a buck, boomerangs . . ."

"Turn it off," shouted Woody. "Someone's going to hear."

The TV blared, "Banjos for a buck, buck, buck!" Al flapped his chicken wings. "And that's cheap, cheap, cheap!" A map flashed on the screen, and Al pointed to the Toy Barn.

Hamm waddled forward, grabbed the remote, and turned off the TV. "I despise that chicken," he complained.

Slinky inched his wiry silver body into the room. "Okay," he gasped, out of breath. "I got good news and I got bad news."

"What, what?" asked the toys.

"Good news is, I found Woody's hat!" Slinky wagged his tail—upon which Woody's hat was perched.

"My hat!" shouted Woody. "Aw, Slink . . . thank you! Thank you!"

"What's the bad news?" asked Buzz.

"Here it comes!" shouted Slinky.

Chapter Three

A sniffing sound pierced through the low chatter. It got louder, and then even louder, and then it turned into a bark.

"Aaah! It's Buster," shouted Rex.

The toys all rushed to the door in an attempt to block out the inevitable. Rocky strained, but the pressure was too great. The dog's wet nose nudged through the crack in the door. And the toys knew it wasn't stopping there.

"Woody! Hide! Quick!" called Bo.

With a yelp, Woody dived into Andy's duffel bag, and burrowed underneath some clothes and a baseball mitt. Suddenly the door creaked open.

Buster, a caramel-colored dachshund,

11

jumped triumphantly to the center of the room. He barked loudly and ran around the room, scattering toys and drool everywhere.

Etch spun quickly, in order to avoid Buster. But Buster, noticing the movement, pounced, flattening him. Buster panted, and looked around. Drool dripped from his mouth, and he continued his rampage.

As soon as Buster moved on, Etch wobbled to a standing position. The remains of his picture were covered with paw prints.

Suddenly Buster sniffed and turned toward the pile of bags. He ran over to the duffel, pulled Woody out, and flung him. Woody landed in the center of the room, lifeless.

Buster jumped on top of Woody, lips curled. He growled for a second, and then began to lick him.

"Okay, okay," sputtered Woody. "You found me, Buster. All right. Hey, how'd he do that, Hamm?"

Hamm stood in front of Mr. Spell's readout of 13.5 seconds. "Eh, looks like a new record!"

Woody snapped his fingers. "Okay, boy. Sit. Stick 'em up! Pow!"

With a happy yelp, Buster fell over and played dead.

"Great job, boy," said Woody, scratching Buster's belly. "Who's gonna miss me while I'm gone? Who's gonna miss me?"

Suddenly, voices from the hallway drifted into Andy's bedroom.

"Andy? Have you got all your stuff?" asked Andy's mom, Mrs. Davis.

"It's in my room," said Andy.

Woody gasped and ran off to take his position. All of the other toys froze where they were, and lay lifeless.

Andy kicked his bedroom door open wide with one cowboy boot. He walked in, revealing his full cowboy outfit. Buster barked and ran to Andy. "Stick 'em up," shouted Andy, pulling his toy guns out of their holster on his belt.

Buster left the room, and headed down the stairs.

"I guess we'll work on that later," Andy said, putting down his toy guns. He walked up to Woody, who was propped up on his bag. "Hey, Woody. Ready to go to cowboy camp?"

"Andy, honey," called his mother. "Five minutes and we're leaving."

Andy began to play with Woody. He picked up Buzz, too. They began to shake hands, but to Andy's shock and dismay, Woody's arm ripped!

"Andy, let's go," called Mrs. Davis. She poked her head into Andy's room. "What's wrong?" she asked.

"Woody's arm ripped!" gasped Andy.

"Maybe we can fix him on the way?" Mrs. Davis suggested.

"No, let's just leave him," sighed Andy, tossing Woody aside.

"I'm sorry, honey. But you know, toys don't last forever." Mrs. Davis placed Woody on the highest shelf in Andy's room, amidst a pile of old books. Then she and Andy left the room.

Seconds later, the toys came back to life. They stared up at Woody. "What just happened?" they questioned.

"Woody's been shelved," cried Mr. Potato Head.

Woody scrambled to the edge of his shelf and looked out the window. Andy and his mother were getting into their van. Sadly he watched as the van pulled away.

Chapter Four

It was a long, hot summer on the shelf. The sun rose early one August morning. Woody was shaken from his sleep by the sound of a van pulling up in front of the house. Once more, he looked out the window.

Andy jumped out of the car, riding a hobbyhorse. "Yee-haw! Ride 'em, cowboy! Whoa! Yeah! Giddyap! Giddyap!"

"He's back," Woody whispered. He glanced down. Rex, Slinky, Mr. Potato Head, and Rocky were sitting and playing cards at the foot of the bed. "Hey, everybody! Andy's back! He's back early from cowboy camp!"

They heard Andy bound up the steps.

"Places everyone! Andy's coming," yelled Hamm.

The toys dropped their cards and scattered. Woody froze in his "toy pose" just as Andy burst into the room. Andy ran up to Woody and pulled him down from the shelf. "Hey, Woody! Did you miss me?"

"Giddyap, giddyap. Ride 'em, cowboy!" Andy walked Woody across the floor, and swung his arms. Suddenly, Andy's smile faded. "Oh, I forgot," he said to Woody. "You're broken." He stared at Woody, frowning. "I don't want to play with you anymore." And with that, Andy dropped Woody.

Woody landed, forlorn, in a trash can filled with broken toy parts. Struggling, he tried to crawl out of the can. "Andy!" he yelled, struggling as toy arms pulled him back to the bottom of the can.

Andy stared into the can. "Bye, Woody!" He closed the lid.

Woody woke up with a start. He was still on Andy's shelf. "Huh? What's going on?" He glanced around the room, confused. Until he realized that it had all been a bad dream. He got up, and his broken arm bumped into a pile of books, knocking them over. A pile of dust rose, and Woody coughed. Soon he noticed that he wasn't the only one coughing. "What's going on? Wheezy, is that you?" he said to a small stuffed penguin.

"Hey, Woody," gasped Wheezy.

"What are you doing up here? I thought Mom took you to get your squeaker fixed months ago. Andy was so upset . . ." said Woody, confused.

"Nah," said Wheezy, motioning with one fuzzy wing. "She just told Andy that to calm him down. Then she shelved me."

"Why didn't you yell for help?" asked Woody.

"I tried squeaking," shrugged Wheezy. "But I'm still broken. No one could hear me." Wheezy squinted his eyes, and tried to squeak. The only sound that emerged was a pathetic, wavery little yelp. He coughed again and explained, "The dust aggravates my condition. Cough, hack, wheeze!" Wheezy fell into Woody's arms, exhausted.

"What's the point of prolonging the inevitable," Wheezy gasped. "We're all just one stitch away from here . . . to there." He pointed outside.

Woody looked out the window and gasped. Mrs. Davis was pounding a YARD SALE sign into the ground.

Chapter Five

Woody called down to the other toys. "Yard sale! Yard sale! Wake up, everyone! There's a yard sale outside!"

Buzz and Slinky stirred from their snooze. "Huh?" asked Slinky, stretching out his coiled body.

"Yard sale?" questioned Buzz.

Sharky, Snake, and Troll all popped their heads out of Andy's toy chest.

"Sarge! Emergency roll call," said Woody.

Sarge burst out from the "Bucket-O-Soldiers," saluting Woody.

"Sir! Yes, sir!" He went around to gather all of the toys. "Red alert!" he called through his minimicrophone. "All civilians fall into position! NOW!"

The toys responded quickly, and lined up. "Single file! Let's move, move, move!"

Buzz marched over and began to write on the magic slate.

"Hamm?" he called.

"Here," Hamm shouted.

"Potato Head, Mr. and Mrs.?"

"Here," said Mrs. Potato Head.

Buzz continued the roll call. "Slinky?"

"Yo."

Rex quivered. "Oh, I hate yard sales."

Suddenly there was a bump from behind Andy's door. "Ahh, someone's coming!" Rex warned everyone.

The toys resumed their old positions and froze. Woody hid Wheezy back behind the ABC book on the shelf. Woody returned to his old place as soon as the door began to creak open.

Mrs. Davis entered with a box marked 25 CENTS. She dug under Andy's bed, and placed a pair of blue-and-silver Velcro shoes in the box. She picked up Rex, who tried to hide his look of utter panic. Luckily, she placed Rex on a table. She was merely moving him to get to the puzzle that he was sitting on. Next she reached up to the top shelf where Woody and

19

Wheezy were, and took the ABC book. Woody sighed, but seconds later, Mrs. Davis reached for Wheezy. "HSSSS . . . HSSSS" squeaked Wheezy, as he was dropped into the box. "Bye, Woody," he whispered, as he was carried out of the room.

Woody gasped. "Not Wheezy. Oh, c'mon, think, Woody, think . . . think." He had to do something. Woody raised his good arm, and let out a loud whistle. Buster came bounding into the room. "Here, boy. Here, Buster, up here!" called Woody.

He tried to climb down, but slipped because of his bad arm. He began to fall toward the hardwood floor. Buster scrambled toward Woody, and was able to catch him at the last second.

"Ooof!" groaned Woody. He propped himself up on Buster's back, and patted his matted fur. "Okay, boy, to the yard sale."

"Did he say yard sale?" Mr. Potato Head asked the others.

"He's crazy!" agreed the toys.

Chapter Six

Out on the front lawn, Woody and Buster hid behind an armchair at the edge of the yard sale. They peered around the chair, checking to see if the coast was clear. "Okay, boy," Woody whispered into Buster's ear. "Let's go, boy. And keep it casual."

They inched their way over toward the table with the 25 CENTS box. Buster paused at the edge of the table, and Woody jumped on. He hid for a moment behind a tall pepper grinder. Then, he ran over to the box, hoisted himself up, and jumped inside.

Seconds later, Woody was able to recover Wheezy. He pushed Wheezy up and over the edge of the box, and then jumped out himself.

They both ran to Buster. Woody tucked Wheezy into Buster's collar. "There you go, pal."

"Bless you, Woody," wheezed Wheezy.

"All right now, back to Andy's room, where we belong," Woody said, as he climbed onto Buster's back himself.

"Way to go, cowboy!" yelled the other toys, who were watching from the window.

They bounced back to victory, but Wheezy started to slip out from under Buster's collar. "Woody . . . I'm slip'n . . . oh, oh," he chanted with each bounce.

Woody held on to Wheezy with his good arm. But when Buster had to jump over a skateboard in their path, Woody was thrown to the ground. The oblivious hound kept on running, leaving Woody flat on his back in the grass.

Woody lifted his head, and watched Buster and Wheezy make their way back into the house. He groaned, but indeed, the worst was yet to come.

"Mommy, mommy! Look at this!" yelled a little girl. Her body cast a large shadow over Woody. "It's a cowboy dolly . . ."

Back in Andy's room, the toys watched the

scene in horror. Buzz looked through the binoculars. "No, no, no . . ."

"That's not her toy!" shouted Rex.

"What does that little gal think she's doing?" asked Slinky.

The girl picked up Woody and ran to her mother. "Mommy, can we keep him? Please?"

"Oh, honey, we're not going to buy any broken toys," her mother said, staring at Woody's limp arm. She took Woody from her daughter and placed him on a nearby table.

Mrs. Davis didn't notice, but someone else did. A big man with a goatee gasped and ran over to Woody. "Original hand-painted face, natural dyed blanket-stitched vest . . ." He picked up Woody and grinned. "Hmmm, a little rip . . . fixable. Oh, if only you had your hand-stitched polyvinyl—" The man suddenly spotted Woody's hat on the ground.

"Hat!" he yelped. "Oh, I found him! I found him! I found him!"

Mrs. Davis walked over to the man. "Excuse me. Can I help you?" she asked.

He looked up. "Oh, ah, I'll give you, ah, fifty cents for all this junk."

"Oh, now, how did this get here?" said Mrs. Davis, reaching for Woody.

"Oh, a pro," laughed the man. "Very well . . . five dollars."

"I'm sorry." Mrs. Davis shook her head. "It's an old family toy." She took Woody from the man and began to walk away.

He got out his wallet and followed Mrs. Davis. "Wait, wait! I'll give you fifty bucks for him!" he said, waving the cash in front of Mrs. Davis.

"He's not for sale," she answered.

"Everything's for sale," reasoned the man. "Or, or trade . . . Ummm, you like my watch?"

"Sorry," said Mrs. Davis, shaking her head. She put Woody in the cash box and locked it.

The man lurked around the yard sale, waiting for the perfect moment when Mrs. Davis would be distracted. When she turned her back, he pried open the cash box and grabbed Woody. Hiding Woody in his suitcase, he ran to his car. He dropped the bag into the backseat through the open window, got in the car quickly, and took off . . . tires screeching as he tore down the street.

Woody bounced around inside the suitcase. Shaken and terrified, he wondered how he was going to get back to Andy. Woody heard the car stop and the door open, and then he was lifted out. He unzipped the bag and peered out. He noticed a sign and shuddered.

The sign read NO CHILDREN ALLOWED.

Chapter Seven

Back in Andy's room, the toys gathered around to plan a way to get Woody back. Hamm stood in front of Etch, pacing.

"All right," he said. "Let's review this one more time." He tapped his pointer on the Etch A Sketch, where Woody's figure was drawn. "At precisely 8:32-ish, Exhibit A, Woody, was kidnapped. The composite sketch of the kidnapper . . ."

Etch quickly erased Woody, and then drew a short fat guy with a beard that almost touched his feet, it was so long.

"He didn't have a beard like that," protested Bo.

"Fine," said Hamm. "Etch, give him a shave."

Etch erased the man, and drew another one, without the beard.

"The kidnapper was bigger than that," said Slinky.

"I know he wore glasses," said Bo.

"Yeah, he's too small," the other toys agreed.

"Oh, picky, picky, picky," complained Hamm.

"Just go straight to Exhibit F!" said an impatient Mr. Potato Head.

Exhibit F was a street and traffic scene constructed out of Lincoln Logs. Pointing to a matchbox car, Mr. Potato Head traced the route of the car. "The kidnapper's vehicle fled the scene in this direction."

"Your eyes are on backward," said Hamm. "It went the other way."

"Excuse me. A little quiet please," said Buzz. He was studying Mr. Spell, whose screen was lit up with the letters: LZTYBRN.

The toys approached Buzz. "What are you doing?" asked Rex.

"I managed to catch the license plate of the car Woody was taken in. There's some sort of message encoded on that vehicle's ID tag."

Mr. Spell gave some suggestions. "Lazy,

Toy, Brain. Lousy, Try, Brian. Liz, Try Bran."

"It's just a license plate . . . it's just a jumble of letters," said Mr. Potato Head.

"Yeah, and there are about 3.5 million registered cars in the tricounty area alone," said Hamm, turning back to the Etch A Sketch.

"Lazy, Try, Brian," Mr. Spell continued.

"Oh, this can't help. Let's just leave Buzz to play with his toys," said Mr. Potato Head.

The other toys started to retreat, when Buzz cracked the code.

"Toy, toy, toy!" he yelled.

"Al's Toy Barn," said Mr. Spell.

"Al's Toy Barn!" they all repeated.

Buzz spun around and ran to Etch. "Draw that man in the chicken suit!" he said.

When Etch finished the drawing, the toys stared in amazement. "It's the chicken man!" gasped Rex.

"That's our guy," said Buzz.

"I knew there was something I didn't like about that chicken!" said Hamm.

Chapter Eight

Al stomped into his apartment in full chicken suit gear. He grabbed his cell phone and started yelling into it. "Yeah, yeah, yeah. I'll be right there. And we're gonna do this commercial in one take, do you hear me? Because I am in the middle of something really important!" He hung up and stared at Woody, who was now trapped behind a glass case.

"You, my little cowboy friend, are going to make me big . . ." He began to flap his wings. "Buck, buck, bucks," he finished, laughing.

When Al left the room, Woody rammed his shoulder into the door of the case. After a few pushes, he was able to open it. He jumped to the floor and rushed over to the door. The front door was way out of reach, and he couldn't open it. Instead, he jumped up to a chair and onto the windowsill.

Woody gasped when he got a glimpse outside. There were tall buildings everywhere, and it was clear that he was far from home. "Andy," he sighed, wistfully.

Woody jumped down from the windowsill and began to explore Al's apartment. Suddenly, a floppy toy horse slipped through his legs. "Whoa-oa-oa!" yelled Woody, as the horse leaped around like a bucking bronco. Woody struggled to hang on. "Hey, stop! Horsy, stop! Sit, boy! Whoa! Sit, I say!"

The horse sat down, causing Woody to tumble to the floor. His legs flipped over his head. He was upside down when he noticed a cowgirl doll standing in front of him. "Yee-haw!" she yelled, and grabbed Woody, straightening him. "It's you! It's you!" She gave him a big noogie. "It's really you!"

"What's me?" asked Woody.

"Whoo-wee!" exclaimed the cowgirl. She spun Woody around like a swing dancer, and held on to his pull string. She yanked him back, and caught him with her other arm. Then she put her ear to his chest to listen. "There's a snake in my boot!" said Woody's voice box.

30

"Ha!" said the cowgirl, slapping Woody on the back. "It is you!"

"Please stop saying that," pleaded Woody. "What is going on here?"

"Say hello to Prospector," said the cowgirl. She whistled to the horse, who dived into the cardboard box, dug around, and pulled out an old miner doll, wrapped in his own original plastic casing. "You remember the Prospector, don't you?" she asked.

"Oh, we've waited countless years for this day! It's so good to see you, Woody," said the Prospector, who was dressed in mining clothes and had a plastic pick hanging from his belt.

"Listen, I don't know what . . . Hey! How did you know my name?" asked Woody.

"Everyone knows your name, Woody," said the cowgirl.

"You mean, you don't know who we are?" asked the Prospector. "Bullseye?" he said.

Bullseye the horse galloped up on to the boxes, and turned on the lights. Woody glanced around the room and gasped. He was surrounded by the complete set: "Woody's Roundup Collection."

There were boxes of toys: a tractor, the

horse, and an entire ranch. There was a Woody yo-yo, a cereal box, and even a magazine cover with a close-up of Woody's face.

Prospector nodded at Bullseye, and the horse pushed a videotape into the VCR. Jessie turned on the TV with the remote. A pair of barn doors flashed on the screen. The title card read COWBOY CRUNCHIES PRESENTS.

The TV announcer boomed, "Cowboy Crunchies, the only cereal that's sugar-frosted and dipped in chocolate, proudly presents . . . *Woody's Roundup*! Starring Jessie, the yodeling cowgirl!"

A doll just like the cowgirl danced onto the screen. "Yo-de-lay-he-hoo!" she bellowed.

A mass of animals fell from the sky—skunks, rabbits, armadillos, a squirrel—surrounding Jessie. They squealed and squeaked.

"Look! That's me," shouted Jessie. She jumped up and down and pointed at the screen enthusiastically.

Woody stared from the screen to Jessie, confused.

The TV announcer continued, "The sharpest horse in the West . . ." as Bullseye galloped on screen.

"Stinky Pete, the Prospector!" On screen,

the Prospector emerged from a cardboard mine. "Has anyone seen my pick?" he asked.

The Prospector smiled at Woody. "The best is yet to come," he whispered, nodding to the screen.

"And the high-ridin'est, rootin' tootin'est hero of all time—Sheriff Woody!"

Woody watched as his onstage self burst forward, leaped onto Bullseye, and reared up.

"Hey howdy hey, Sheriff Woody," shouted the audience of kids. Dozens of them were wearing cowboy hats, waving and cheering at their hero.

As the facts came together for Woody, his shock turned to joy. He had once been a big star.

Chapter Nine

Back at Andy's house, the toys gathered around the TV. They went from channel to channel, searching for the Al's Toy Barn commercial. When they found it, Etch quickly sketched a copy of the map, placing a bold "X" on the spot that marked the Toy Barn.

"That's where I need to go!" announced Buzz, pointing at the X.

"You can't go alone," said Rex. "You'll never make it there."

"Woody once risked his life to save me. I couldn't call myself his friend if I weren't willing to do the same," explained Buzz. "So who's with me?" He glanced around the room.

Mrs. Potato Head filled Mr. Potato Head's rear compartment with attachments. "I'm packing you an extra pair of shoes, and your *angry* eyes, just in case," she said to him.

Bo grabbed Buzz and kissed him on the cheek. "This is for Woody—when you find him," she said.

Buzz blushed. "All right, but I don't think it'll mean the same . . . coming from me."

Slinky, Mr. Potato Head, Rex, Buzz, and Hamm walked across the rooftop toward the edge. Mr. Potato Head grabbed the end of Slinky's coil, and jumped off the roof, using Slinky as a bungee cord. "Geronimo!" he yelled, as he landed safely on the lawn below.

Hamm jumped next, and then Rex. Buzz walked back to the window. "We'll be back before Andy gets home," he told the others.

The toys inside gathered at the window and waved good-bye. "To Al's Toy Barn—and beyond!" yelled Buzz, as he leaped off the roof. Slinky jumped last. The search for Woody had begun!

Chapter Ten

Woody walked around Al's apartment in awe. "I can't believe I had my own show!" he marveled. Jessie and Bullseye followed him around. Prospector watched from his box in the corner.

"Didn't ya know? Why, you're valuable property!" said Jessie.

"Oh, I wish the guys could see this. Hey howdy hey—that's me! I'm a yo-yo!" he said, picking up the yo-yo with his face on it, and giving it a spin. Next he walked over to "Woody's Ball Toss" and threw a ball, knocking out his front teeth. He put some coins in the Roundup bank, and then played with the bubble machine. "What . . . you push the hat, and out comes . . . Oh, out come bubbles!

Clever." Woody was getting used to the idea, and he liked it.

Bullseye popped the bubbles with his mouth as they came out. Jessie laughed.

Woody continued to explore, picking up a boot. He looked inside, and a spring snake jumped out, smacking him in the face. "Aha, I get it! There's a snake in my boot."

"Check this out, Woody," said Jessie. She put on the Woody record player, and it cranked out old Western music. Bullseye and Jessie began to dance around, and Woody joined them. "Hop on, cowgirl!" said Woody, as he jumped onto the record player. The record spun him around. He jumped up to avoid the needle arm. Jessie joined him, jumping in time. "Not bad," said Woody.

"Wooo-eee!" shouted Jessie. "Look at us! We're a complete set!"

"Now it's on to the museum," said Prospector.

"Museum?" asked Woody. He stopped short, causing all of them to trip over the needle of the record player. They flew across the room and landed in a heap on the shelf. "What museum?" groaned Woody.

"We're being sold to the Konishi Toy Museum in Tokyo," explained Prospector.

"That's in Japan!" added Jessie.

"Japan? I can't go to Japan," said Woody, standing up and brushing the dust from his knees.

"What do you mean?" asked Jessie, straightening her pigtails.

"I gotta get back home to my owner—Andy. Look, see?" Woody raised his boot and pointed to the name ANDY, which was etched on his sole.

"You still have an owner?" gasped Jessie.

"Oh, my goodness . . ." said Prospector, scratching his head.

"I can't do storage again. I won't go back into the dark," started Jessie, pacing back and forth.

"Jessie, it's okay!" said Prospector, as Jessie started to wave her arms frantically.

"What's the matter? What's wrong with her?" asked Woody.

Jessie was crying in the corner. Prospector explained. "Well, we've been waiting in storage for a long time, Woody. Waiting for you."

"Why me?" asked Woody.

"The museum's only interested in the collection if you're in it, Woody. Without you, we go back into storage. It's that simple."

"It's not fair!" cried Jessie. "How can you do this to us?"

"Hey, look." Woody put his arms up and backed away. "I'm sorry but this is all a big mistake. See, I was in this yard sale and—"

"Yard sale?" said Prospector. "Why were you in a yard sale if you have an owner?"

"Oh, I wasn't supposed to be there," Woody explained.

"Is it because you're damaged? Did this Andy break you?" asked Prospector.

Woody cradled his arm in defense. "Yes, but . . . no, no, no . . . it was an accident. He—"

"Sounds like he really loves you," snapped Jessie.

"It's not like that, okay!" shouted Woody. "I'm not going to any museum."

Suddenly the door creaked open. "Al's coming," warned Prospector. The Roundup Gang scrambled to their original positions.

Seconds later, Al was in the room. He bent down and grabbed a camera out of a box. "Oh, ho, ho, ho . . . money, baby," laughed Al. He pulled out Bullseye and Jessie and arranged them in front of the Roundup barn for a shot. "Money, money, money. And now, the main attraction." He grabbed Woody from his case. But Woody's arm got caught on the stand and it tore off. Al noticed after he sat Woody down on the stand. "Aaaaah! His arm. Where's his arm?" he yelled.

Al found it on the ground, grabbed it, and tried to reattach it to Woody's shoulder. "What am I going to do?" he asked. "Oh, I know." Al put Woody down on a chair and then reached for the phone. "Hey, it's me—Al. I got an emergency here," he barked into the phone. "It's got to be done tonight . . . all right, all right. But first thing in the morning. Grrr." Al slammed the phone into its cradle and stomped out of the room, slamming the door behind him.

Woody came back to life. "It's gone!" he said, horrified. "I can't believe it. My arm is completely gone!"

"Awright, come here," said Prospector. "Let me see that. Oh, it's just a popped seam. You should consider yourself lucky."

"Lucky! Are you shrink-wrapped?" said Woody. "I'm missing my arm!"

Jessie slumped in one corner. "Let him go. I'm sure his precious Andy is dying to play with a one-armed cowboy doll."

"Why, Jessie," reasoned Prospector, "you know he wouldn't last an hour out there in his condition. It's a dangerous world out there for a toy."

Chapter Eleven

Buzz leaped out of a pile of shrubs, sneaking between pools of streetlamp light. Finally, he took cover behind a mailbox at the corner. He looked back and motioned for the others to follow him.

Rex jumped out of the shrub first, camouflaged in leaves. As he ran to Buzz, all but one of the leaves fell to the ground. "Oh." He laughed. "This is just like when my invisibility shield wore off on Level Fourteen . . . I was completely exposed! Well! I made an earnest attempt to hide . . ."

Slinky, Potato Head, and Hamm appeared next, scurrying along quickly. Hamm tripped over a crack, and his cork fell out. Coins clanged to the ground. "Oow. Ooof. All right, nobody look till I get my cork back in," he cried.

"So then Zurg annihilated me with his ion blaster!" continued Rex.

"Oh, not the video game again," cried Mr. Potato Head. He popped his ears out so he wouldn't have to listen to Rex anymore.

Buzz looked down at the map. "Good work, men. One block down and only nineteen more to go," he said.

"Nineteen!" cried the other toys.

"Are we gonna do this all night? My parts are killing me," said Mr. Potato Head.

Buzz waved his arm. "Come on, fellas. Did Woody give up when Sid had me strapped to a rocket?"

"No!" yelled the others.

"No! And did he give up when you threw him out of the back of that moving van?" asked Buzz.

"Oh, you had to bring that up," said Mr. Potato Head.

"We have a friend in need and until he's safe in Andy's room we will not rest. Now let's move out!" Buzz marched down the street, and the other toys followed him.

Chapter Twelve

The sun rose over Andy's neighborhood. Buzz and the gang were still on their way to the rescue. "Hey, Buzz, can we slow down?" asked Hamm. "May I remind you that some of us are carrying over six dollars in change."

"Losing health units . . . must . . . rest," panted Rex.

Buzz stopped, and waited for Hamm, Mr. Potato Head, Rex, and Slinky to catch up to him. "Is everyone present and accounted for?" he asked.

"Not quite everyone," said Mr. Potato Head.

"Who's behind?" asked Buzz.

"Mine," said Slinky, whose back end was trailing far behind.

"Hey, guys!" said Hamm. "Why did the toys cross the road?"

"Not now, Hamm," said Buzz.

"Ooh! I love riddles. Why?" asked Rex.

"To get to the chicken on the other side!" Hamm answered. He pointed. Al's Toy Barn was directly across the street. A giant chicken loomed in front.

"Hurray! The chicken!" shouted Rex.

Horns honked, and a huge truck rumbled by, shooting a crushed soda can toward the toys.

They ducked, and scrambled out of the way. They stared at the busy road in front of them and shivered. "Oh, well. We tried," said Rex, inching away from the street.

Buzz grabbed him by the tail. "We'll have to cross," he said.

"You're not turning me into mashed potato!" said Mr. Potato Head.

"I may not be a smart dog," said Slinky. "But I know what roadkill is!"

Buzz surveyed the scene. He spotted some orange cones, and rubbed his hands together. "I have an idea!"

A minute later, each toy was securely under an orange cone at the edge of the road.

"Okay, here's our chance! Ready, set, go!"

The cones began to move across the street. Some cars sped in front of them. "Drop!" warned Buzz. All of the cones dropped. "Go!" he shouted, when it was clear. The cones hurried forward. Cars veered out of their way, and before long, they were safely on the other side of the street.

"Good job, troops," said Buzz. "We're that much closer to Woody!"

The toys headed toward Al's Toy Barn. When they got close, they noticed a large sign that read CLOSED.

"Oh, no. It's closed," cried Slinky.

"We're not preschool toys, Slinky. We can read," said Mr. Potato Head.

"Shhh," said Rex. "Someone's coming." The toys hid under a shopping cart as a workman approached. He stepped on the black mat in front of the electronic doors and they slid open.

"Hey, Joe, you're late! We've got a ton of toys to unload in the back. Let's get going," said another workman from inside the store.

"All right, I'm coming . . . I'm coming," said Joe.

The toys glanced at each other. Buzz nodded. "All right, let's go," he said.

"But the sign says it's closed," said Rex.

Everyone ignored him, and stood on the mat. Finally, Rex followed, shaking his head, but nothing happened. The doors remained closed.

"C'mon, open!" said Hamm. But still the doors stayed closed.

"No, no, no," said Buzz. "All together."

The toys watched as he counted off with his head. "Now!" Buzz yelled, and all the toys jumped at once. When they landed, the doors whooshed open and they stepped inside.

Al's Toy Barn was huge. Thousands upon thousands of toys lined the walls. "Whooaa, Nellie! How're we gonna find Woody in this place?" asked Slinky.

"Look for Al," said Buzz. "We find Al, we find Woody. Now, move out!"

The toys scattered in search of Woody.

Buzz turned a corner and came face-to-face with an entire aisle of Buzz Lightyear boxes. He stared in awe. "Wow . . ." He stepped forward to examine the toys more closely. A bright green glow captured his attention. A large cardboard sign read NOW WITH UTILITY BELT.

"I could use one of those," marveled Buzz.

He climbed to the top of the display case, and reached for the belt. Before he was able to grab it, he spotted a giant pair of moon boots. He glanced up. Towering over him was the new Buzz Lightyear.

Meanwhile, Rex and Mr. Potato Head were exploring a different aisle. Rex was ecstatic. He had found a book called *Defeat Zurg*. He couldn't stop talking about it. In fact, he was talking so much that Mr. Potato Head popped his ears off so he wouldn't have to hear any more of his ramblings.

Suddenly, a red car careened down the aisle toward Rex and Mr. Potato Head. It screeched to a halt beside them, revealing its driver and passenger, Hamm and Slinky.

"Eh, I thought we could search in style," said Hamm.

"Nice going there, Hamm. So, how 'bout letting a toy with fingers drive?" said Mr. Potato Head.

Hamm moved over, and Mr. Potato Head took the steering wheel. They drove off, ramming into the occasional shelf. Rex continued to babble on, but no one was paying attention.

Meanwhile, Andy's Buzz circled the New Buzz, sizing him up. He checked out his own reflection in New Buzz's shiny helmet glass. "Am I really that fat?" he wondered. Andy's Buzz spied the utility belt, and reached for it.

"Ho-yahhh!" yelled New Buzz, putting Andy's Buzz's arm in a lock. He pointed to hundreds of other Buzz Lightyears still in their boxes.

"Oww! What are you doing?" complained Andy's Buzz.

"You're in direct violation of code six-four-oh-four-point-five, stating all Space Rangers are to be in hyper-sleep until awakened by authorized personnel," barked New Buzz in a stiff, computerlike voice.

"Oh, no," said Andy's Buzz.

New Buzz spun Andy's Buzz around, pushing him up against the display. "You're breaking ranks, Ranger," he said.

New Buzz kicked Andy's Buzz's legs apart and put him in an armlock. He opened his wrist communicator, distracted.

"Buzz Lightyear to Star Command. I've got an AWOL Space Ranger."

"Tell me I wasn't this deluded," complained Buzz, rolling his eyes.

"No back talk," warned New Buzz. "I have a laser and I will use it."

"You mean the laser that's a lightbulb?" teased Buzz, as he pressed the laser.

New Buzz gasped. "Has your mind been melded? You could've killed me, Space Ranger. Or should I say, 'Traitor'?"

Buzz broke free. "I don't have time for this," he said.

New Buzz raised his laser and aimed it at Buzz's head. "Halt! I order you to halt!"

Buzz dropped from the podium to the floor. New Buzz jumped on his back, tackling him. They began to wrestle. Buzz got New Buzz into an armlock, and then pushed him into the Buzz Lightyear Pin Screen.

Rex read from his *Defeat Zurg* manual. "Wow! It says how you defeat Zurg! Look!" Rex placed the book in front of the windshield so everyone could see. But now no one could see where they were going. The car swerved, and the other toys screamed.

"Rex! Watch it! Look out! We can't see!" they yelled.

The car was headed directly into a giant box of Superballs. "Look out!" yelled Slinky.

The car grazed the side of the box, and the Superballs spilled, cascading wildly to the ground. It created a blizzard of multicolored rubber. Balls bounced off of everything, including the car, Mr. Potato Head, and Hamm. Everyone yelled as the car spun around wildly.

Rex's *Defeat Zurg* manual flew out of the car. "My source of power!" he yelled, jumping out of the car and racing after the book. It slid under a shelf, lost. "Where'd it go? No! Come back!" He watched the car speed away. "Wait up! Dinosaur overboard!" Rex chased after the car.

Meanwhile, Buzz had been overtaken by New Buzz. New Buzz shoved Buzz into an empty box, and used the packaging wires to secure him.

"Ow!" said Buzz. "Listen to me! You're not really a Space Ranger! You're a toy! We're all toys! Do you hear me?"

New Buzz slid Buzz into a box and closed the cardboard container. "Well, that should hold you until the court-martial!"

"Let me go!" Buzz pleaded from the box.

New Buzz turned and left just as the other toys pulled up to him.

"Hey, Buzz," said Hamm.

New Buzz turned, took aim, and fired his

laser at the toys. "Halt!" he shouted. "Who goes there?"

"Quit clowning around and get in the car," said Mr. Potato Head.

"Buzz! Buzz! I know how to defeat Zurg!" said Rex.

"You do?" asked New Buzz.

"C'mon, I'll tell you about it on the way," said Rex.

Buzz watched from the shelf, horrified. "No, no, guys! You've got the wrong Buzz!"

"Say, were'd ya get that cool belt, Buzz?" asked Hamm.

"Well, slotted pig, they're standard issue," said New Buzz. He got in the car and they drove away.

Buzz yelled from the box, but no one could hear him.

Chapter Thirteen

A flash went off, blinding Woody momentarily. He was propped up on his stand. The rest of the Roundup Gang was set up around him. *Flash, flash, flash* . . . Al fanned through his new pictures with a huge smile on his face. "It's like printing my own money!" he exclaimed. The phone rang and Al picked it up. "Yeah, what?" he shouted. "Oh, oh, Mr. Konishi. I have the pictures right here. In fact, I'm in the car right now, on my way to the office to fax them to you. I'm going through the tunnel," he lied. "I'm breaking up." He made some garbled sounds and then hung up the phone.

As soon as Al left the room, Woody leaped from his stand. "Oh, wow! Will you look at me! It's like I'm fresh out of the box!" Woody admired his fixed arm. Someone had come to sew him up and clean him. He admired his new stitching. "Will you look at this! Andy's gonna have a hard time ripping this!" Woody waved his new arm wildly in front of the other toys' faces. "Hello! Hi! Hello!"

Woody admired himself in the reflection of the cellophane of Prospector's box.

Jessie frowned and walked away. "Great, now you can go," she said.

"Well, what a good idea," said Woody. He walked to the edge of the table and looked at the heating grate below. Bullseye nudged him from behind. Woody stared into his sad eyes.

"Woody, don't be mad at Jessie," said Prospector. "She's been through more than you know. Why not make amends before you leave, huh? It's the least you can do."

Woody sighed. "All right. But I don't know what good it'll do." He went over to Jessie, who was hugging her knees and staring out the window.

"Look, Jessie. I know you hate me for leaving, but I have to go back. I'm still Andy's toy. Well, if you knew him, you'd understand. You see, Andy's a real . . ."

"Let me guess," Jessie interrupted. "Andy's a real special kid, and to him, you're his buddy, his best friend; and when Andy plays with you, it's like, even though you're not moving, you feel like you're alive—because that's how he sees you."

"How did you know?" asked Woody. He was truly stunned.

Jessie stared at Woody. "Because Emily was just the same. She was my whole world." Jessie started to cry. She buried her head in her hands. Her voice came out muffled. "You never forget kids like Emily, or Andy, but they forget you," she sobbed.

"Jessie, I . . . I didn't know," said Woody.

"Just go," she said.

Woody reluctantly slumped off. He jumped off of the sill to the floor, and walked back to the grate where the Prospector and Bullseye stood. Woody opened the grate and stared down at the ventilation shaft. He glanced back at Jessie.

"How long will it last, Woody?" asked Prospector. "Do you really think Andy is going to take you to college? Or on his honeymoon? Andy's growing up and there's nothing you can do about it. It's your choice,

Woody. You can go back, or you can stay with us and be adored by children for generations. You'll live forever."

Woody let go of the grate and spun around. "Who am I to break up the Roundup Gang?" he said. Bullseye licked his hand, and Prospector smiled. Woody and Jessie grinned at each other.

Chapter Fourteen

The toys rummaged through the desk and drawers at Al's office.

"Woody, are you in here?" asked Hamm.

"Woody?" they called.

Rex approached New Buzz. "You see, all along we thought that the way into Zurg's fortress was through the main gate. But in fact, the secret entrance is to the left, hidden in the shadows."

New Buzz turned. "To the left and in the shadows. Got it."

They heard Al enter the office and they hid.

Al turned on his fax machine as he talked into his cell phone. "Yeah, there was a big pileup, but I don't want to bore you with the details. Now, let me confirm your fax number. All right, slower. That's a lot of numbers. I got it."

"It's him," whispered Slinky.

"The chicken man," said Hamm.

"Funny, he doesn't look like poultry," said New Buzz.

"That's the kidnapper, all right," said Slinky.

"An agent of Zurg if I ever saw one," said New Buzz.

"And the pièce de résistance," Al said, as he slid a picture of Woody through the fax. "I promise the collection will be the crown jewel of your museum!" The photo went through the machine and popped out the other side, falling to the floor near where the toys hid.

"Woody!" they gasped.

"Now that I have your attention, imagine we added another zero to the price, huh? What? Yes? Yes! You've got a deal!" Al yelled. "I'll be on the next flight to Japan!"

"He's selling Woody to a toy museum," whispered Mr. Potato Head.

"In Japan!" said Rex.

New Buzz pushed everyone into Al's bag.

"Into the poultry man's cargo unit. He'll lead us to Zurg. Move, move, move!"

Al laughed like a maniac. "I'm gonna be rich! Rich! Rich!" he bellowed, picking up his bag as the last of the toys slipped in. Rex's tail hung out the back of the bag.

Chapter Fifteen

Back at the toy store, Buzz had managed to shift his box sideways on the shelf. With each shove against the plastic, he moved another inch. He teetered over the edge, and finally dropped to the floor. He kicked open the bottom of the box, then struggled with the arm restraints. He jerked his right arm hard and broke free. He untied the rest of his body, and crawled out of the box, kicking it in disgust.

Buzz heard Al coming down the aisle and hid. He peered around the corner after Al turned and noticed Rex's tail sticking out of the back of the bag that Al carried. Buzz raced down a parallel aisle, trying to catch up to his friends. He was almost in the clear when he slipped on some loose Superballs left over from the crash. Buzz recovered quickly, and crawled up the display case. Swinging like a gymnast, he jumped onto a trampoline.

When he bounced high enough, Buzz dove for the closing electric doors in desperation . . . and smacked right into the glass. "Ooph!" yelled Buzz. He jumped up and down on the electric sensor on the doormat, but the door just wouldn't budge. Buzz looked around and spotted a large stack of boxes by the door. He kicked the bottom box out, causing the entire pile to topple over. The door opened with their weight, and Buzz ran toward it. Buzz ran out the door, chasing after Al.

Buzz didn't notice that when the electronic doors closed, the top of one of the boxes ripped open. Zurg crawled out, and then whipped his head toward Buzz. His red eyes glowered and his claws clenched as he watched Buzz. His deep mechanical voice growled, "Destroy Buzz Lightyear . . . Destroy Buzz Lightyear." Set free, Zurg followed Buzz's trail.

Chapter Sixteen

The toys heard Al cut the engine. He got out of the car, slamming the door behind him.

"He didn't take the bag!" said Rex, as he watched from inside.

New Buzz hopped over Rex and jumped out. "No time to lose," he said. He tried the door handle, but couldn't get it open.

They all watched Al get in the elevator. "He's ascending in the vertical transporter," said New Buzz. He opened his wings and grabbed on to Rex and Mr. Potato Head. "All right, everyone! Hang on! We're going to blast through the roof!"

"Uh, Buzz," said Rex.

"To infinity and beyond!" boomed New Buzz.

"What are you, insane?" asked Mr. Potato Head. He noticed the door lock next to the window, and ran up Rex's back so he could reach it. "Stand still, Godzilla," he said. Mr. Potato Head strained to lift the lock.

New Buzz scratched his head and leaned against the electric window switch. "I don't understand. Somehow my fuel cells have gone dry . . ."

Ka-chunk! Suddenly the lock popped open, tearing off Mr. Potato Head's arms. He sailed through the air and bounced off of Slinky's head. "Ahhh!" he yelled. He finally landed upside down in the cup holder.

The car door opened and New Buzz ran out. He watched through the glass doors as the elevator needle stopped at the penthouse. "Blast!" cried New Buzz. "He's on Level Twenty-three."

"How are we gonna get up there?" asked Slinky.

Rex looked up. "Maybe if we find some balloons, we could float to the top. . . ."

The others looked at him in surprise. "Are you kidding?" asked Mr. Potato Head. "I say we stack ourselves up, push the intercom, and pretend we're delivering a pizza!"

"How about a ham sandwich?" asked Hamm. He glanced at Mr. Potato Head and Slinky. "With fries and a hot dog?"

"What about me?" asked Rex.

"Eh, you can be the toy that comes with the meal," shrugged Hamm.

"Troops! Over here," said New Buzz.

They all turned to see New Buzz taking the cover off of an air vent. "Just like you said, Lizard Man—in the shadows, to the left. Okay, let's move!"

The toys followed New Buzz into the duct. New Buzz spoke into his wrist communicator. "Mission Log—have infiltrated enemy territory without detection and are making our way through the bowels of Zurg's fortress."

Hamm turned to the others. "You know, I think that Buzz aisle went to his head," he whispered. The others nodded, but they all followed him through the shaft.

Soon after, they came to a crossroads. Slinky looked in both directions. "Oh, no . . . which way do we go?" he asked.

"This way," said New Buzz, running forward.

"What makes you so sure?" asked Mr. Potato Head.

"I'm Buzz Lightyear. I'm always sure!"

"Woody's been shelved!"

The other toys watch as Woody is kidnapped!

"It's you!" exclaims Jessie.

A rescue plan is hatched . . .

. . . and the search begins!

Woody can't believe what a big star he was!

Woody teaches Jessie and Bullseye how to play.

"We're being sold to the Konishi Toy Museum in Tokyo," explains the Prospector.

"I gotta get back home to my owner—Andy. Look, see?"

"Go!" Buzz shouts.

New Buzz begins to scale the walls.

"See, that's me!" says Woody.

"You—are—a—toy!" exclaims Buzz.

"It's Zurg!"
yells Rex.

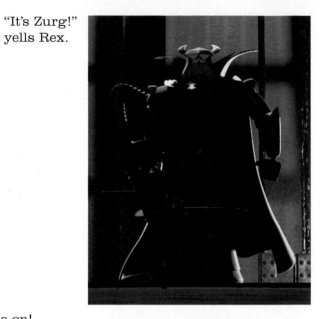

The chase is on!

A noise echoed throughout the duct. "We've been detected," said New Buzz. "The walls! They're closing in." New Buzz grabbed Mr. Potato Head and lifted him overhead. "Quick! Help me prop up Vegetable Man, or we're done for!" he said.

"Put me down, you moron!" cried Mr. Potato Head.

"Hey, guys, look! It's not the walls, it's the elevator," said Rex. He pointed to a different duct, where they caught sight of the elevator heading down.

They walked to the elevator shaft and peered up. New Buzz put on his suction cup gloves and reeled out a line and hook. "Come on," he said. "We've got no time to lose." He handed out the line. "Everyone grab hold."

"Huh?" asked the others.

"Hey, uh, Buzz?" asked Hamm. "Why don't we just take the elevator?"

New Buzz began to scale the walls. "They'll be expecting that," he explained.

Meanwhile, a weary and frustrated Buzz made it to the front of Al's apartment building. He noticed a trail of footprints in the soft grass, leading to the vent. He ducked down and followed the trail.

Chapter Seventeen

Al paced back and forth in his living room, yelling into his phone once more. "To overnight six packages to Japan is how much? What? That's in yen, right? Dollars? Doh! You are deliberately taking advantage of people in a hurry, you know that? All right, I don't . . . I'll do it! All right, fine!"

He stacked a bunch of boxes onto a cart with wheels and headed out the door with it. "I'll have the stuff waiting in the lobby and you'd better be here in fifteen minutes, because I have a plane to catch. Do you hear me?"

The Roundup Gang was packed into their boxes. But they weren't being shipped to Japan. They were going on the plane with Al in his carry-on case.

When Al left the apartment, Woody, Jessie, and Bullseye sat up.

"Woo-hoo!" yelled Jessie. "We're finally going! Can you believe it?"

Bullseye sniffed excitedly and then snuggled into his thick foam packaging.

Prospector chuckled. "That's custom-fitted foam insulation you'll be riding in, Bullseye. First-class stuff, all the way!"

"You know what?" said Woody. "I'm actually excited about this. I mean it. I really am."

Jessie jumped next to Woody, and they began to square dance. "Yee-haw! Swing yer partner, doh-see-doh. . . . Look at you, dancin' cowboy," she said.

Bullseye clapped his hooves. Prospector glided his box back and forth. "Look! I'm doing the box step!" he cried.

Chapter Eighteen

Thock, thock, thock. New Buzz climbed the wall slowly, pulling the others behind him.

Hamm grunted. He tilted and some of his change began to drop out of his coin slot. "Uh-oh . . . Hey, heads up down there," he called.

"Whoa! Pork bellies are falling," said Slinky.

Some coins landed on Mr. Potato Head's face. "Hey," he yelled. "Not much farther, Buzz?" he asked, hopefully.

"My arms can't hold on much longer," complained Rex. The elevator shaft shuddered, causing Rex to slide down the line. He bumped into the other toys, and pushed them down with him. In the end, they were all desperately clinging to the bottom of the towline.

"Buzz, help!" called Slinky.

"Too . . . heavy . . ." panted New Buzz. Suddenly, he got an idea. "What was I thinking? My antigravity servos!" He pushed a button on his utility belt.

"Hurry up, Buzz," said Hamm.

"Hang tight, everyone," said New Buzz. "I'm going to let go of the wall."

"What!" the toys cried.

"He wouldn't," said Mr. Potato Head.

"One," said Buzz.

"He would," said Hamm.

"Two," he called.

"For the love of . . . no!"

"Three," called New Buzz. He pushed off of the wall and went into his flying pose. He looked up, his fist jutting forward. They were frozen in space for a second. And then . . . they plummeted down, landing on the top of the elevator as it was rising.

"To infinity and beyond," called New Buzz, unaware that his attempt at flying had failed.

The elevator began to slow down. "Approaching new destination. Reengaging gravity," New Buzz said. The others looked at each other and rolled their eyes. The elevator stopped right at the airshaft at the twenty-third floor. New Buzz leaped into the vent and scanned the area. "Area secure," he reported to the others.

They groaned and panted as they climbed into the vent.

"It's okay, troops. The antigravity sickness will wear off momentarily. Now . . . let's move!" said Buzz.

"Remind me to glue his helmet shut when we get back," Mr. Potato Head whispered to Hamm.

Once inside the vent, New Buzz spoke into his wrist communicator again. "Have reached Zurg's command deck, but no sign of him, or his wooden captive."

Suddenly, Woody's voice echoed through the chambers. "That's Woody!" said Slinky.

The toys turned and ran down the duct. They reached the grate to Al's apartment in a few seconds, and they tried to peer through.

Woody was being tickled by Jessie, but his friends could only hear his voice. "I'm begging you! No more! I'm begging you, stop. Please!" he shouted.

"Buzz, can you see what's going on?" asked Mr. Potato Head.

New Buzz lifted one of Mr. Potato Head's eyes up to the slats in the vent. "What's happening?"

Mr. Potato Head gasped. "It's horrible! They're torturing him!"

"What are we going to do, Buzz?" asked Rex.

"Use your head," said New Buzz.

The toys grabbed Rex, and aimed his head at the door. Using him as a battering ram, they scrambled forward. "But I don't want to use my head," cried Rex.

"CHARGE!" they all yelled.

Woody had left the grate unscrewed, so the stampeding toys caused the grate to fall down even before they reached it. Unable to stop, they all sped into the room, passing the Roundup Gang and smashing into the far wall.

Everyone yelled.

"What's going on here?" asked Prospector.

"Guys!" cried Woody. "Hey, how did you find me?"

"We're here to spring you, Woody," explained Slinky.

Andy's toys rushed the Roundup Gang.

"Hold it, now! Hey, you don't understand! These are my friends," said Woody.

"Yeah, we're his friends," said Rex, puffing his chest out.

"Well, not you—them," said Woody, nodding at the Roundup Gang.

Slinky quickly circled around Jessie and Bullseye, tying them up with his coils.

"Hey," said Jessie.

"Grab Woody and let's go," said Slinky.

New Buzz ran to Woody, picked him up, and started to carry him off.

"Fellas, hold it!" Woody protested. "Hey, Buzz—put me down."

"They're stealing him!" cried Jessie.

The toys rushed the vent, but Andy's Buzz was blocking it. "Hold it right there!" he said.

"Buzz?" said Woody and Andy's other toys.

"You again?" asked New Buzz.

Buzz looked up at Woody, who was still in New Buzz's arms. "Woody, thank goodness you're all right."

"Buzz, what's going on?" asked Woody.

New Buzz dropped Woody. "Hold on a minute. I am Buzz Lightyear, and I'm in charge of this detachment."

"No, I'm Buzz Lightyear," said Buzz to the others.

"So who's the real Buzz?" asked Woody.

"I am," they both said.

New Buzz turned to the others. "Don't let this imposter fool you. He's probably been trained by Zurg himself to mimic my every move."

Buzz reached over and popped New Buzz's helmet open. New Buzz sputtered and gasped for air, falling to the ground.

While New Buzz faltered, Buzz calmly lifted his foot and showed everyone the ANDY written in the sole.

"I had a feeling it was you, Buzz," said Slinky. "My front end just had to catch up to my back end."

Rex looked from one Buzz to the other. "You know, now that I really look I can see the difference."

New Buzz managed to close his helmet and stand up. "Will someone please explain what's going on?" he asked.

"It's all right, Space Ranger," said Buzz. "It's a code five-four-six."

"You mean it's a . . ." said New Buzz.

"Yes," said Buzz.

"And he's a . . ." said New Buzz.

"Yes," said Buzz.

New Buzz rushed over to Woody and bowed down on one knee. "Your majesty," he said.

Woody looked down, confused.

Buzz took Woody's arm. "Woody, you're in danger here. We need to leave now."

"Al's selling you to a toy museum, in Japan!" said Rex.

"I know, it's okay," said Woody, pulling away. "I actually want to go."

"What? Are you crazy?" asked Mr. Potato Head.

"The thing is," explained Woody, "I'm a rare Sheriff Woody doll, and these guys are my Roundup Gang." He motioned to Jessie, Bullseye, and Prospector, who waved.

"What are you talking about?" asked Mr. Potato Head.

"*Woody's Roundup!* It's this great old TV show, and I was the star!"

Wood clicked the remote and the TV and VCR turned on with the show playing in the middle of an episode.

"See, now look . . . Look at me! See, that's me!" said Woody.

On the screen, the TV Woody was riding

the TV Bullseye toward a cliff. TV Jessie fell off, and they caught her.

Andy's toys watched in amazement.

"This is weirdin' me out," said Hamm.

Woody explained, "Buzz, it was a national phenomenon. And there was all this merchandise that just got packed up. You should see it. There was a record player, a cereal box, and a yo-yo. Buzz, I was a yo-yo."

"Was?" questioned Mr. Potato Head.

Buzz pulled Woody aside. "Woody, stop this nonsense and let's go."

"I can't go. I can't abandon these guys. Without me the set's incomplete. They'll go back into storage—maybe forever. They need me to get into the museum."

Buzz raised his voice. "You—Are—A—Toy! You're not a collector's item. You are a child's plaything."

"For how much longer?" reasoned Woody. "One more rip and Andy's done with me. What do I do then, Buzz, huh? You tell me."

"Woody, the point is being there for Andy when he needs us," said Buzz. "You taught me that. That's why we came all this way to get you."

"Well, you wasted your time," sighed Woody.

Buzz and Woody stared at each other for a minute.

Buzz turned toward the grate. "Let's go, everyone," he said.

"What about Woody?" asked Slinky.

"He's not coming with us," said Buzz.

"But, but, Andy's coming home tonight," said Rex.

"Then we'd better make sure we're there waiting for him," said Buzz.

Buzz held the vent open for the rest of Andy's toys and New Buzz. They glanced at Woody sadly before filing out, and then disappearing into the darkness. Buzz paused.

"I don't have a choice, Buzz," said Woody, shrugging his shoulders. "This museum . . . it's my only chance."

"To do what, Woody?" asked Buzz. "Watch children from behind glass? Some life." He jumped into the vent, and closed the grate behind him.

Woody stared at the closed grate as the Roundup Gang toys approached him.

"Good going, Woody. I thought they'd never leave," said Prospector.

Woody wandered over to the TV to watch the end of the episode. The TV Woody was singing. The song trickled in through the grate, and Andy's toys paused to listen for a moment.

On the TV screen, a shy little boy was pushed onto the stage. He slowly approached TV Woody. The boy hugged TV Woody with all his might.

Woody looked down at the sole of his shoe. He scratched away the new paint until the name ANDY showed through. Woody got up. "What am I doing?" he said. He ran past the Roundup Gang, heading straight for the vent.

"W-Woody? Where are you going?" asked Prospector.

"You're right, Prospector. I can't stop Andy from growing up, but I wouldn't miss it for the world!"

"No!" gasped Jessie and Prospector.

"Buzz, Buzz," yelled Woody, running through the vent.

Both Buzzes turned. "Yes?" they asked.

"Wait! I'm coming with you!" Woody said.

Andy's toys cheered.

"Wait for me," said Woody. "I'll be back in just a second." He turned on his boot heel and headed back toward Al's apartment.

Chapter Nineteen

Woody rushed back into Al's apartment. "Hey, you guys!" he called to the Roundup Gang. "Come with me!"

Jessie, Bullseye, and Prospector stared at Woody in surprise.

"Look," said Woody. "I know I won't be played with forever, but Buzz is right. Today I still have Andy, and today I know he'd play with all of us."

"Woody, I . . . I don't know," stuttered Jessie.

"Wouldn't you give anything just to have one more day with Emily?" asked Woody. "Well, here's your chance! Come on! Take it!" Woody glanced at Bullseye. "Are you with me?" he asked.

Bullseye eagerly licked Woody's face.

"Good boy. Good boy. Prospector, how about you?" Woody turned to Prospector's box, but it was empty.

Woody's eyes opened wide with terror. Prospector had slammed the grate shut and was using his plastic pick like a power tool to spin the screws tight.

Jessie gasped.

"You're outta your box?" asked Woody, horrified.

"I tried reasoning with you, Woody," said Prospector. He finished tightening the screws and walked back to his box. "But you keep forcing me to take extreme measures."

Woody started to protest, but Prospector raised his hand to silence him. "Look, we have an eternity to spend together in the museum. Let's not start off by pointing fingers, shall we?"

"Prospector! This isn't fair," said Jessie.

"Fair," said Prospector. "I'll tell you what's not FAIR. Spending a lifetime on a dime-store shelf, watching every other toy be sold. Well, finally my waiting has paid off, and no hand-me-down cowboy doll is gonna screw it up for me now!" Prospector flung his box into the special packing case and then climbed in himself.

Woody ran to the vent, pulling on the grate. "Help! Help! Buzz! Guys!" he screamed.

"It's too late," called Prospector. "That silly Buzz Lightweight can't help you."

"His name is Buzz Lightyear!" shouted Woody.

"Whatever," said Prospector, closing the lid of his box.

Andy's toys raced down the vent toward the grate. They struggled to open it, but it wouldn't budge.

"It's stuck," called Woody.

The two Buzzes began slamming into it. "Should I use my head?" offered Rex.

The lock on Al's apartment door began to rattle. Jessie and Bullseye jumped into their cases as the door creaked open. Woody had no choice but to join the rest of the Roundup Gang.

"Ah! Look at the time. I'm gonna be late," growled Al.

Andy's toys watched in horror as Woody was taken away.

"Quick! To the elevator," cried Buzz.

The toys raced down the duct.

Chapter Twenty

Riding on top of the elevator was Zurg. "All too easy," he muttered, as Buzz Lightyear came into view.

"It's Zurg!" yelled Rex. "Watch out, he's got an ion blaster."

Zurg fired at New Buzz, who jumped into action. New Buzz leaped over Zurg, and moved swiftly to avoid all of his assaults.

Zurg whipped his body around and fired his ion balls. *Pop, pop, pop.*

New Buzz ducked for cover behind a generator box.

Meanwhile, Al got into the elevator with the Roundup Gang in tow.

As the elevator descended, New Buzz and Zurg began to fistfight.

"Quick, get on," cried Buzz. The toys jumped onto the elevator roof. They watched New Buzz's struggle. Zurg lifted him overhead, and threw him to the ground.

"Surrender, Buzz Lightyear. I have won," boomed Zurg.

"I'll never give in. You killed my father," said New Buzz.

"No, Buzz . . . I am your father," said Zurg.

"NO-O-O!" screamed New Buzz.

Rex scrambled down from the top of the elevator and ran up behind Zurg. "Buzz, you could have defeated Zurg all along. You just need to believe in yourself!" said Rex.

Zurg raised his blaster to New Buzz's head. "Prepare to die!" shouted Zurg.

"Ahh, I can't look," said Rex, covering his eyes. As he turned away, his tail knocked Zurg off balance. Zurg fell, rolled to the edge of the elevator shaft, and then fell down, plunging into the darkness.

"AAHHHH!" yelled Zurg.

Rex peered over the edge of the elevator shaft. "I did it! I finally defeated Zurg!"

New Buzz joined Rex and looked down. "Father?"

Meanwhile, Slinky dangled down into the

elevator, and managed to unlock Al's case, freeing Woody. They grabbed hold of each other as the elevator touched down to the lobby. Slinky pulled Woody from one end, but Prospector pulled from the other, forcing Woody back into the case.

Al exited the elevator, taking Woody with him. The toys followed.

"How are we gonna get him now?" asked Rex.

Mr. Potato Head pointed to an idling Pizza Planet truck. "Pizza, anyone?" he asked. Everyone smiled and headed toward the truck.

Buzz noticed New Buzz falling behind. "Are you coming?" he asked.

New Buzz carried a lifeless Zurg in his arms. "No. I must bury my father, and fill out the proper forms." They waved good-bye, and New Buzz walked back to Al's Toy Barn.

The toys climbed into the truck and Buzz took control of the situation. "Slink, take the pedals. Rex, you navigate." He slid a stack of pizza boxes under the steering wheel. "Hamm and Potato, operate the levers and knobs."

Inside the truck, three tiny green aliens

hung from the rearview mirror. "Strangers, from the outside," they said.

"Oh, no!" moaned Buzz.

Rex pointed. "He's at the red light. We can catch him."

"Maximum power, Slink," Buzz ordered.

Slinky pushed on the gas pedal with all of his might. The truck wouldn't budge. On the dashboard, Rex peered through the windshield. "It turned green. Hurry up!"

"Why won't it go?" asked Buzz.

The aliens pointed to the stick shift. "Use the wand of power," they said.

Standing on top of Hamm, Mr. Potato Head struggled to get the car into gear. He jammed the gears hard and the truck sped forward.

"Ahh!" yelled Rex, as the truck hit a line of orange cones.

"Rex, which way?" asked Old Buzz.

"Right. I mean left. No, no, right . . . I mean *your* right!" said Rex.

The truck sped down the street, swerving wildly.

Al's car turned. "There he is!" shouted Rex. "He's turning left!"

Buzz cranked the steering wheel, and the

truck cut across three lanes of traffic. The aliens swung on a string and flew across the car, heading out the window. Mr. Potato Head leaned out and grabbed them just in time.

"Buzz! Go right! To the right! Right!" shouted Rex.

The truck turned again, and Mr. Potato Head and the aliens whipped back into the truck, safely.

"You saved our lives!" chanted the aliens. "We are forever in your debt."

Mr. Potato Head slapped his forehead and groaned.

The toys sped into the airport, parking in the unloading area. "There he is!" said Buzz, pointing to Al. He was checking his case with the ticket agent.

The toys sneaked up behind Al, hidden in a pet carrier. "Once we get through, we just need to find that case," said Buzz. The pet carrier was checked, and the toys rode down the conveyor belt with the bags. When the carrier tumbled onto the lower conveyor belt, it burst open, freeing the toys.

Slinky spied Al's case first. "There it is!" he yelled, pointing to the right.

"No, there's the case!" said Hamm, pointing to the left.

"You take that one, and we'll take this one," said Buzz.

Hamm, Rex, and Mr. Potato Head ran to the case on the left. They unzipped it, only to find a jumble of camera equipment.

Buzz chased after the case on the right and kicked open the latch. "Okay, Woody, let's go!" he called. Buzz reached into the case and opened it, only to be punched and knocked off of the belt by Prospector.

Prospector climbed out and waved his plastic pick at Buzz. "Take that, space toy!"

Suddenly Woody popped up beside Prospector and grabbed him in a headlock. "Hey! No one does that to my friend!"

In their struggle, both toys fell out of the case. Prospector slashed Woody's arm with his pick, and it ripped open once more.

"Your choice, Woody!" growled Prospector. "You can go to Japan together . . . or in pieces! If he fixed you once, he can fix you again! Now, get in the box."

"Never," said Woody.

Prospector raised his pick to land one final blow, when he was blinded by light.

Snap, snap, snap. Andy's toys shot Prospector with the cameras, distracting him with the flashing.

"Gotcha!" yelled Buzz, grabbing Prospector.

"Fools!" sputtered Prospector. "Children will destroy you! You'll be ruined! Forgotten! Thrown away . . . spending eternity decomposing in some rotten landfill!"

"Well, Stinky Pete, I think it's time you learned the true meaning of *playtime*," said Woody. "Right over there, guys."

"No!" gasped Prospector, as they stuffed him into a child's backpack. "You can't do this to me! Noooo!"

"Hi!" said one of the dolls inside. Prospector looked up, startled. He turned the other way to find another doll.

"You'll like Amy," said another doll. "She's an artist."

Prospector was surrounded by six dolls in various states of design. Scattered in the bag with them were crayons, scissors, and paintbrushes.

Prospector screamed as the case made its way along on the conveyor belt.

Buzz and Woody waved. "Happy trails, Prospector," called Woody.

"Hey, Woody," said Hamm. "We can't get Jessie out." The case was approaching the end of the line, and Jessie was stuck inside.

"Woody! Help!" she yelled. Still in the case, Jessie plummeted down a steep belt ramp. The toys watched in horror as a baggage handler closed the case, loaded it onto a tram, and drove off.

Woody whistled, and Bullseye galloped forward. Woody and Buzz jumped on and took off in pursuit of Jessie. "Ride like the wind, Bullseye," Woody yelled. Bullseye reared up and took off.

"Yee-ha! Giddy-up!" said Woody.

The three sidled up next to the moving luggage tram. Woody jumped onto the tram, and struggled with the case that contained Jesse. The baggage handlers approached, and Woody had to freeze, watching in horror as the case was loaded onto the plane.

Woody sneaked onto the plane. He found the case and opened it, finding Jessie on top of the foam. "Excuse me, ma'am . . . but I believe you're on the wrong flight."

"Woody!" yelled Jessie.

"Come on, Jess. It's time to take you home." Woody hugged Jessie.

"But, I'm a girl toy," said Jessie.

"Nonsense," said Woody. "Andy will love you. Besides, he's got a little sister."

"He does?" said Jessie. "Well, why didn't you say so? Let's go."

Woody grabbed Jessie's arm and pulled her out of the case. The two ran behind a suitcase, hiding from the baggage handler.

Before they could escape, though, the doors closed.

Buzz and Bullseye stared in disbelief, from the runway below.

"What are we gonna do?" gasped Jessie.

"Come on! Over there!" Woody pointed to some light leaking in from the other end of the cargo hold. They ran over and peered through the opening, at the landing gear below.

"Are you sure about this?" asked Jessie.

"Yes, now go," said Woody. He used his pull string like a lasso, and secured it around a bolt protruding from the landing gear. Woody and Jessie swung down, landing beside Buzz on Bullseye's back. "Yeee-haaa!" yelled Woody. He disconnected his pull string just as the plane picked up speed, escaping just in time.

"We did it!" yelled Jessie. "That was definitely Woody's finest hour!"

"Nice ropin', cowboy," said Buzz. He handed Woody his hat, which had fallen off earlier.

"Let's go home," said Woody.

Chapter Twenty-One

The Davis van pulled up to the house, and stopped. Andy jumped out, and ran toward the front door. He burst into his bedroom, and jumped onto his chair, searching his shelf for Woody. But all he could find were some dusty old books.

Disappointed, he turned and looked around the room. On his bed he saw WELCOME HOME, ANDY spelled out on Etch. Surrounding Etch were all of his toys, plus Jessie and Bullseye. Overjoyed, Andy jumped down from the chair and picked up Woody, Jessie, and Bullseye. "Oh, wow! Thanks, Mom!"

Andy played with his toys. "Woody and the cowgirl fly across the Snake River Canyon . . . Oh, no! They're attacked by a ferocious dinosaur. Rooaar!" said Andy, picking up Rex and mashing him into Bullseye.

"Help, help, somebody! A dinosaur's eatin' my horse!" Andy said, in Jessie's voice.

"Buzz Lightyear flies in to save the day," Andy continued. "Take that, dinosaur," he said, in Buzz's voice.

"Andy, breakfast is ready," called Mrs. Davis.

"Okay, Mom. Be there in a second," yelled Andy. Before Andy left, he wrote his name on the sole of Jessie's boot and Bullseye's hoof, and then ran out.

As soon as he left, Jessie grinned and showed her boot to Bullseye. "Yee-ha!" she said. "We're part of a family again, huh, Bullseye?"

"Ahem," said Buzz, approaching Jessie. "I'd just like to say that your hair . . . it's a lovely shade of . . . yarn . . . uh, I gotta go," he sputtered, turning away.

Jessie lassoed Buzz with her pull string and pulled him closer. "Well, ain't you the sweetest space toy I ever met!" she said.

Woody came up behind them. "Buzz has a girlfriend. Buzz has a girlfriend," he teased. Buzz blushed.

Jessie put her hands on her hips. "He does? Who is she? Well, she's gonna have to get past me!"

Meanwhile, the three aliens looked adoringly at Mr. Potato Head. "You saved our lives," they chanted. "We are eternally grateful."

"You saved their lives?" asked Mrs. Potato Head. "My hero! I'm so proud of you." She gave him a kiss. "And they're so adorable," she said, glancing at the aliens. "Let's adopt them."

"Daddy!" said the aliens.

"Oh, no!" said Mr. Potato Head. He slapped his hand to his forehead and fell backward. His parts came loose as he landed on his back.

Meanwhile, Hamm played the video game. "Hey, Rex, can you give me a hand over here? I need your magic touch," he said.

"I don't need to play. I've lived it," sighed Rex.

Hamm turned off the game. Al's Toy Barn commercial flashed onto the screen.

"Welcome to Al's Toy Barn," said a sobbing TV Al. "We've got the lowest prices in town. Everything for a buck, buck, buck!"

Hamm and Rex watched intently. "Crime doesn't pay!" Hamm said to the TV.

Woody showed Bo his arm, which Andy had fixed with orange yarn. "Andy did a good job, huh? What do you think?"

"I like it," said Bo. "It makes you look tough."

Wheezy waddled over, squeaking.

"Wheezy, you're fixed!" said Woody.

"Oh, yeah. Mr. Shark looked in the toy box and found me an extra squeaker," he said.

"And how do you feel?" asked Woody.

"I feel swell. . . . In fact, I think I feel a song coming on!"

Mr. Microphone tossed Wheezy his mike.

Woody left the festivities and walked over to the far windowsill. Buzz joined him.

"You still worried?" asked Buzz.

"About Andy? No," said Woody. "It'll be fun while it lasts."

"I'm proud of you, cowboy," said Buzz, patting him on the back.

"Besides," said Woody, "when it all ends, I'll have old Buzz Lightyear to keep me company . . . for infinity and beyond!"

Buzz and Woody laughed, and joined their friends.